Figaro

Excitable and ready for adventure, Figaro knows the neighbourhood like the back of his paw.

Pixie

Pixie has a nose for trouble and a very active imagination!

Katsumi

Sleek and sophisticated, Katsumi is quick to call Kitty at the first sign of trouble.

For Inky, the most mischievous cat in town - P.H.

For Helena and her cat crew - J.L.

OXFORD
UNIVERSITY PRESS

Great Clarendon Street, Oxford OX2 6DP

Oxford University Press is a department of the University of Oxford.
It furthers the University's objective of excellence in research, scholarship, and
education by publishing worldwide. Oxford is a registered trade mark of Oxford
University Press in the UK and in certain other countries

British Library Cataloguing in Publication Data

Data available

ISBN: 978-0-19-277166-7

1 3 5 7 9 10 8 6 4 2

Printed in China

Paper used in the production of this book is a natural,
recyclable product made from wood grown in sustainable forests.
The manufacturing process conforms to the environmental
regulations of the country of origin.

Kitty
and the
Tiger Treasure

OXFORD
UNIVERSITY PRESS

Chapter 1

Kitty sprang from the sofa to the door in a single bound. 'Stop right there!' She pointed her finger at Pumpkin the cat. 'You won't get away with it this time!'

Pumpkin, a roly-poly ginger kitten

with little black whiskers, scampered
out of reach. 'Can't catch me!' he
meowed, darting into Kitty's bedroom.

Kitty chased after him, giggling.
Pumpkin leapt onto the bed and rolled
over to let Kitty tickle his fluffy tummy.

Kitty's mum came in. 'What are you two up to? There's a lot of giggling going on in here.'

'We're playing Catch the Baddie!' Kitty told her. 'It's a new game we invented, and it helps me improve my superpowers ready for when I need them.'

'I see!' Mum smoothed back Kitty's dark hair. 'I'm pleased you're practising but it's getting late now. It's time to settle down and go to bed.'

Kitty climbed under her blanket.

'I feel quite sleepy now.'

'I'm not surprised!' Mum smiled as she tucked Kitty in.

Kitty smiled back. She knew her mum understood how important it was to practise her powers. Kitty's family had a special secret. Mum was a real superhero and went out at night to use her cat-like abilities to help people. Kitty and her little brother, Max, had the same superpowers as their mum. Kitty could see in the dark and pick up noises from far away. She could also balance perfectly and perform amazing somersaults. Best of all, she could talk to animals!

A few weeks ago, Kitty had been on her very first night-time adventure. She had met Pumpkin, who had no friends and no place to stay. Kitty was so happy that the ginger kitten had come home with her. Now he was part of the family and he slept on Kitty's bed every night.

'Don't forget we've got a big day tomorrow,' added Mum as she tidied

Kitty's clothes. 'We're going to the Hallam City Museum to see the new exhibition. The Golden Tiger statue will be there, along with lots of other ancient treasures.'

Kitty sat up in bed again. 'Is the Golden Tiger really covered with diamonds?'

'That's right! And it has large emerald eyes,' Mum told her.

'I can't wait to see it!' cried Kitty.

'I'm glad you're excited,' said Mum, laughing. 'Sleep well, honey!'

Kitty turned on her bedside lamp and snuggled down under the covers. She couldn't wait until tomorrow. The new treasures at the museum were meant to be amazing. The Golden Tiger statue was worth a huge amount of money because it was decorated with so many jewels. Kitty couldn't wait to see them all winking and glittering!

Pumpkin padded across the bed and flopped down beside her. His blue eyes shone in the dim light and his fur was velvety-soft against Kitty's arm. Kitty sighed and closed her eyes. Pictures of imaginary treasure floated round her head.

Pumpkin wriggled. 'Kitty, are you asleep?' he whispered.

Kitty's eyes flew open. 'No, I'm not! What's wrong, Pumpkin?'

The kitten's whiskers twitched.

'What's the Golden Tiger statue like? Is it enormous?'

'It looks quite small in the pictures. It's probably no bigger than you!' Kitty smiled.

'Then why is it so special?' asked
Pumpkin.

'Mum says it was buried in an
ancient tomb for thousands of years
before archaeologists found it. It's
painted with gold and decorated with
diamonds, and the tiger's eyes are made
from sparkling emeralds.'

'It must be valuable then.'
Pumpkin snuggled against Kitty's
shoulder.

'It's priceless!' Kitty told him. 'And
it could be magical too. The legend goes

that the Golden Tiger listens to your
heart's desire and, if you touch its paw,
it will grant your greatest wish.'

'Ooh, that sounds mysterious.'
Pumpkin's blue eyes grew wider.

'Dad told me all about it,'
continued Kitty. 'Lots of people have
had good luck after seeing the statue
but there's a curse too. If a baddie
does something terrible that makes the
statue angry it will conjure up ghostly
spirits to seek revenge!'

Pumpkin shivered. 'Ooh—spooky!'

'I hope I get close enough to see it properly tomorrow. The new exhibition is opening for the first time so I think the place will be quite crowded.'

'I wish I could come with you!' said Pumpkin. 'Are cats allowed to visit?'

Kitty shook her head. 'I don't think so. It's not really fair!' She lay quietly for a moment. Then she sat up so suddenly that she nearly knocked Pumpkin off the bed. 'I've got a great idea! If we visit the museum tonight then you'll be able to see everything

and there'll be no crowds at all. We'll
have the whole place to ourselves!'

Pumpkin's nose twitched. 'But . . .
is the museum very creepy?'

'It's full of interesting things. We
can look at them together.' Kitty tickled
Pumpkin under the chin. She knew
the little ginger cat got nervous about
new things and new places. After all,
he was only a kitten and he'd been all
alone before he met
Kitty. 'Don't you think
it would be fun to have a

new adventure?'

Pumpkin nodded slowly. 'I like the sound of the statue with the diamonds and emeralds. Jewels are so sparkly, aren't they?'

Kitty pushed back the covers and jumped out of bed. 'We should go right now! The museum is only ten minutes away and I can use my superpowers to find a way across the rooftops.'

Pumpkin sprang onto the window seat and pushed back the curtain with his nose.

A crescent moon
shone brightly, and silvery
light poured into the room. Kitty felt
excitement bubble inside her like a
glass of lemonade. She gazed at the
roofs of the houses all laid
out in long rows.

She could see a way among the chimney pots as if it was a secret path and she was the only one who knew it!

Pumpkin twitched his nose again. 'I just hope it doesn't rain.'

'If it does I'm sure we'll find somewhere to shelter.' Kitty took out her superhero clothes and tied on her black cape and cat tail. Finally, she added her cat ears before looking in the mirror. Dressed in her cat costume, she felt like a proper superhero! Her powers lit up inside her like the moon coming out from behind a cloud.

When she opened the window, the night wind blew in and the curtains flapped. Kitty climbed onto the ledge, her heart skipping. Going out to see the museum's treasures was exciting, and also a tiny bit scary. 'Are you ready, Pumpkin? It's time to start our next adventure!'

Chapter 2

Kitty climbed from the
window ledge to the roof and ran
lightly along the rooftop. The stars
shimmered like diamonds in the
evening sky. Kitty breathed deeply. On
a magical night, with the moon shining

brightly, her superpowers felt stronger
than ever. She turned a cartwheel,
feeling her powers tingling through her
body.

'Do you know the way to the
museum, Kitty?' asked Pumpkin,
climbing up beside her.

Kitty gazed over the rooftops, her special night vision sharpening her eyes. 'Yes, I'm sure I do. Look, there it is, on Crown Street.' She pointed to a tall building made of pale stone. It had a domed roof and huge columns on each side of the front door.

Pumpkin and Kitty ran along the roof and round the chimney pot. Kitty's cape flew out behind her as she leapt from one house to the next. The wind swirled around, making the trees sway, and the shadows of the branches danced in the moonlight.

Suddenly, a sleek black cat with a white face and paws stepped out from behind a chimney pot. Kitty recognized her friend, Figaro, straightaway. 'Hello, Figaro! What are you doing here?'

'Waiting for you of course!'

Figaro twirled his whiskers. 'I spied you climbing out of your window and I thought to myself: what sort of adventure will Kitty embark on today?'

'We're going to the City Museum to see the Golden Tiger statue in the new exhibition,' explained Kitty.

'We want to see it before the crowds come tomorrow.' Pumpkin waved his ginger tail excitedly.

'The statue of the Golden Tiger is a rare and mysterious object!' Figaro's eyes gleamed. 'I have heard the strange legends about its powers.'

'Would you like to come with us?' asked Kitty.

'I would be delighted, dear Kitty.'

Figaro bowed his head. 'Lead the way!'

Kitty led them across the rooftops to Crown Street where the museum stood. She gazed around the museum roof, which was flat around the edges with a glassy dome in the middle. The museum was enormous, with doors and windows on every side.

'I wonder where the Golden Tiger statue will be.' Kitty clambered down to the nearest ledge and peered through the window. There was a row of ancient swords inside a glass cabinet.

She climbed to the next window and gazed at the china vases and silver plates inside the display cases.

Pumpkin stayed close to Kitty while Figaro stepped gracefully from ledge to ledge. Kitty peered into each dark room. The museum was so vast. Where would the Golden Tiger be? At last, she spotted a shiny banner: *Come to see the Ancient Treasures of the Inca World!* Following the arrow, she leapt to the next window ledge and gazed eagerly inside.

The Golden Tiger stood on a small platform, which was surrounded by a red velvet rope. A spotlight shone directly onto the statue, and the tiger's emerald eyes glowed so brightly that for a moment Kitty wondered if it was alive. The Golden Tiger was sitting upright with one paw raised in the air. It was painted gold all over with elegant black stripes across its back and a coat encrusted with diamonds.

'Wow!' cried Pumpkin. 'It looks amazing.'

'I must say it's very impressive.' Figaro swished his black tail. 'Very impressive indeed!'

Kitty pressed her nose to the
window. The shelves around the statue
were loaded with treasures but the
Golden Tiger was the shiniest and most
amazing one of all. 'I'd love to get a bit
closer. Then I could find out whether
the statue really does grant a wish when
you touch its paw!'

'What would you wish for, Kitty?'
asked Pumpkin.

'I don't know!' Kitty bit her lip.
'The jewels on those treasures look
so beautiful. I'd love some diamonds,

emeralds and rubies of my own!'

Pumpkin rubbed his ginger head against Kitty's knee fondly.

'I believe a closer inspection of the statue is an excellent idea,' said Figaro. 'I can think of many things I would wish for: some pampering at the beauty salon, or a four-course meal at Sinclair's Finest Fish Restaurant! Let us go inside at once.'

Kitty hesitated. 'But do you really think we should? No one's supposed to go in there at night.'

'Please, Kitty!' Pumpkin turned his big blue eyes on her. 'I promise I won't touch anything.'

Kitty nodded. 'All right—but we must be really careful.' She spotted an open window on the next floor down. 'There's a way in over here.' She took hold of a drainpipe, ready to climb to the ledge below.

There was a whooshing noise overhead.

'MEEOOOW!' A creature landed heavily on Kitty's shoulder.

Kitty wobbled, grabbing
the drainpipe to keep her balance.

Pumpkin panicked and leapt
on Kitty's foot, pinning it to the
ledge with his paws. 'Eek!
Don't worry, I've got you!'

The creature, a grey Persian cat with bright blue eyes, sprang on to the ledge and stared up at Kitty fiercely. 'You won't get away with this!' she hissed. 'I can spot a cat burglar when I see one. You've come to steal from the museum, haven't you? Well, I won't let you!'

Kitty stared back in surprise.

Who was this new cat and why did she think they were burglars?

Chapter 3

The grey cat flicked her tail
crossly. 'I'm the museum cat and
I won't let anyone get away with
stealing.' She glanced at Figaro and
Pumpkin. 'And you two should be
ashamed of yourselves for helping her.

No true cat would do such a thing!'

Figaro's sleek black-and-white fur bristled. 'What a cheek! How dare you accuse us of being common burglars?'

'Hush, Figaro! It's all right.' Kitty turned to the grey cat. 'You don't need to worry. We're not here to steal anything. We only came to look at the Golden Tiger statue because we were so excited to see it. My name's Kitty and I have superpowers.'

'Oh yes, I've heard about you.' The grey cat studied Kitty's cape and cat ears. Then she bowed her head. 'My name's Cleo. Sorry I jumped on you just now.'

'You should be *very* sorry!' Figaro scowled deeply. 'Fancy landing on someone like that! It's hardly civilized.'

'I got the wrong idea when I saw you sneaking along the window ledge,' said Cleo. 'I hope I didn't frighten you all.'

'Don't worry—we're fine!' Kitty told the grey cat. 'I suppose we must have looked a bit suspicious.'

Figaro made a *humph* sound and turned away to wash his paws.

Pumpkin crept along the ledge to gaze at Cleo with curious eyes. 'Do you really live here in the museum?'

'I sleep in an office at the back of the building,' explained Cleo. 'It really belongs to Stan, the official night-time guard, but he's fallen asleep in his chair

just as he always does. So it's up to me to keep the museum safe. There are a lot of precious things here now the new exhibition has arrived.'

'It sounds like you should be the museum's official guard,' Kitty told her.

Cleo rubbed her ear with her paw. 'I'd love to be a proper guard but the humans don't seem to notice how hard I work. But I love living here—it's amazing! Would you like me to show you around?'

'Yes, please!' Kitty's eyes shone.

'And we'd love to look at the Golden Tiger.'

'It's a very special statue,' said Cleo proudly. 'It looks even better when you're closer. I'll take you inside—just make sure you don't touch anything.'

'What's that funny shadow over the Golden Tiger?' Pumpkin asked suddenly. 'I can hardly see the statue any more.'

'There's a spotlight shining on the statue so it should be easy to see.' Kitty peered through the window. Pumpkin

was right. There was a shadow there . . .
and it was moving!

'It looks so spooky!' squeaked
Pumpkin. 'It's not the curse, is it?'

Kitty pressed her face close to the window. The shadow slipped round the side of the display cabinets and disappeared. Then something, or someone, cut the power to the spotlight. Suddenly the whole room plunged into darkness.

A tingle ran down Kitty's back. 'What's going on? Cleo, something's happening!'

Cleo darted over at once. Figaro stopped washing his paws and joined them.

The moon broke
from behind a cloud, sending
a shaft of moonlight straight through
the dome window. The moving shadow
became clearer. It had a furry brown-and-
white coat and long floppy ears.

'That looks like a springer spaniel.
What's a dog doing in the
museum?' gasped Kitty.

'An intruder!' Cleo's fur stood on end. 'And I was so busy talking that I didn't even notice.'

The dog moved stealthily around the room until it stood right beside the Golden Tiger.

'Paws and whiskers!'

exclaimed Figaro. 'It's heading straight for the statue.'

They watched in alarm as the dog leaned closer and reached out his paw . . .

The dog knocked the statue from its platform. For a second, the Golden Tiger rolled across the museum floor, its diamonds sparkling in the moonlight. The statue's emerald eyes glowed like the eyes of a real tiger. Then the dog picked the statue up in his jaws and ran off into the shadows.

'He's getting away!' squeaked Pumpkin.

Kitty saw the desperate look on Cleo's face. 'Don't worry! We'll help you catch him.' She shinned down the drainpipe to the ledge with the open window.

Kitty thrust the window sash up and leapt inside. The museum was silent and still.

Cleo shook her head. 'Stan must have forgotten to set the burglar alarm again!'

Kitty stared around and shivered. The last time she'd visited the museum, the whole place had been bright and noisy, and full of people.

There was a shadowy shape in the corner and moonlight glinted on something metal. Kitty caught her breath. Then her eyes sharpened and she saw a wax model of an olden-day soldier carrying a spear. She breathed slowly to stop her heart racing. The statue thief was somewhere in the building and she was determined to catch him.

Cleo and Pumpkin tumbled into the room behind her. Figaro climbed in last with a flick of his tail.

'Cleo, can you take us to the exhibition room?' said Kitty.

'This way!' Cleo led them up a grand marble staircase into a splendid room underneath the domed ceiling. Moonlight shone through the window in the top of the dome. All around them, the treasures of the exhibition were laid out in beautiful cases. There were fans painted in delicate colours, coins with strange letters, and silver plates studded with rubies.

A spotlight shone down on the space where the Golden Tiger

had been. Cleo paced around
the platform, her tail swishing.
'I should have noticed!' she
muttered. 'I should have been
watching more carefully.'

Kitty's heart sank as she
stared at the empty platform.

The best treasure of all was missing
and the whole of Hallam City would
be disappointed. Worst of all, what if
the statue really *did* grant wishes? If a
baddie got hold of the Golden Tiger
they might wish for something terrible!

'Look—paw prints!' Pumpkin
pointed at the prints leading away into
the dark.

They followed the paw marks,
which ended at the stairway.

'I fear the trail has gone cold,'
said Figaro, heavily. 'This building

is enormous. We have little hope of finding the scoundrel now.'

'Wait, listen!' Kitty focused with her super hearing. She picked up the sound of paws padding on the floor above. 'He's upstairs! We can still catch him.'

Her heart thumped as she rushed towards the staircase. The race to catch the thief was just beginning!

Chapter 4

Kitty ran lightly up the
spiral stairs and the cats dashed after
her. Cleo's eyes narrowed as they
reached the top. Her grey tail swayed
worriedly and her clear blue eyes
searched the shadowy room.

Kitty heard a creaking sound. 'This way!' she whispered.

At the far end of the gallery, the dog was turning the window catch with his teeth. Kitty crept nearer, her orange trainers noiseless on the polished floor. The robber had put the statue down. Maybe, if they got close enough, they could snatch the Golden Tiger back again.

Pumpkin's ginger tail brushed against a table, knocking over a pile of old coins. They jangled as they rolled

round and round in circles. The dog
whirled round and the moonlight
gleamed on his patchy coat. His
brown eyes were wide and he had a
strange faraway look, like someone in a
daydream.

Kitty shrank into the shadows, raising a finger to her lips. Pumpkin looked like he was about to mew but Figaro clapped a paw over his mouth. The thief gave a low bark before picking up the statue, pushing the window open and squeezing through. Kitty raced to the window and looked along the wide ledge, but the robber dog had already vanished.

Slipping outside, Kitty clambered to the roof. With her super night vision, she scanned the shadowy streets.

Cleo and the other cats scrambled up beside her. Pumpkin twitched his whiskers nervously. Moonlight poured down, sparkling on the museum's glassy dome.

Cleo mewed crossly. 'How could I have been so silly! If I'd been paying attention instead of chatting to all of you then this would never have happened.'

'It's not your fault!' Kitty spotted the dog running down an alleyway. The Golden Tiger gleamed in his jaw. 'Look,

there's the thief! He must have climbed
back inside and made his way to the
ground.' Scrambling to the edge, she got
herself ready to leap across to the roof
opposite.

'Be careful, Kitty!' called Pumpkin.

Kitty felt her superpowers tingling
inside her and her heart skipped with
excitement. She was determined not to
lose sight of the robber dog. She sprang
to the next house and kept on running,
her feet barely touching the rooftop.

Using her outstretched arms to

balance, she leapt from one house to the next. Her cape flew out behind her, as black as midnight. The ground looked far away but she wasn't afraid. She trusted her superpowers. She could do this!

The springer spaniel reached
a row of shops. Kitty edged closer,
ducking behind a chimney pot as the
dog glanced around. A moment later,
he disappeared from view. Cleo and
Pumpkin scampered over to Kitty.

'Where did he go?' whispered Pumpkin.

Figaro puffed a little as he caught up. 'He's obviously a slippery sort of dog. He could be anywhere!'

Kitty crept to the corner of the building and found a metal staircase. 'We can use this fire escape to get down.' She tiptoed down the steps and the cats slipped after her.

The robber dog was hurrying down the street, the statue still clamped in his jaw. He stopped beside a shop, pushed the door open and went inside.

Kitty followed him at a safe
distance. She stared up at the shop sign,
which was lit by a street lamp. 'The
Happy Paws Pet Shop,' she read aloud.
'Do you think he lives there?'

Pumpkin's eyes nearly popped.
'Maybe he's stealing for his owner.'

'Very odd!' said Figaro. 'I haven't
heard much about this pet shop. I think
it only opened a few months ago.'

Cleo sighed heavily. Her grey fur was tinged with orange in the glow of the street light. 'I should have done a better job. I wasn't watching the museum carefully enough. I have to fix this!'

'You *were* doing a good job,' Kitty told her. 'I'm sorry I kept you talking! Let's check the windows and find the best way to get inside.'

'Great idea! If we can take the thief by surprise—' Cleo fell silent as the door opened again.

The robber dog darted outside, his eyes wide and glazed. He scampered down the street and vanished into the gloom.

'He doesn't have the statue any more,' cried Kitty. 'He must have left it inside!'

'There's a way in over there.' Figaro pointed to an open window just below the roof.

'You and Pumpkin should stand guard, ready to warn us if the thief returns,' said Cleo. 'He may be a dangerous kind of dog.'

'Very well!' Figaro nodded. 'Be careful, won't you?'

'Don't worry—we will!' Kitty

scaled the side of the shop and peered
through the window.

It was dark inside and there was a
great deal of shuffling and squeaking as
the animals moved inside their cages.
Kitty slipped through the window.
Then she clambered on to a cupboard
and dropped soundlessly to the floor,
helping Cleo down after her.

Moonlight reflected off the grey
tiled floor. The middle of the shop was
filled with dozens of cages—tall bird
pens, guinea pig and rabbit hutches, and

tortoise cages. Towards the back, shelves of pet food and bedding were hidden in darkness.

'Where do you think he left the treasure?' whispered Kitty.

Cleo sniffed the air. 'It's difficult to follow the trail of his scent. There are too many different animal smells in here.'

'Then we'll just have to search the place.' Kitty looked around for possible hiding places. Then she pointed to the shop counter. 'I'll look over here.' But as she turned, she got a strange feeling that someone was watching her.

A pair of dazzling golden eyes was studying her from behind the pet food shelves.

Kitty's night vision grew sharper and she knew at once that they were cat's eyes. The creature had honey-coloured fur and jewels winked on its collar.

Kitty caught her breath. Who was this new cat and what did they know about the snatching of the Golden Tiger?

Chapter 5

The cat with the strange
golden eyes stared back at Kitty. Then
it vanished, without a word, through a
doorway into a back room.

'Did you see that?' whispered
Kitty. 'We should ask that cat what they

know about the statue.' She turned to Cleo but the grey cat was gone.

Kitty hesitated. Had Cleo been scared away by the other cat? Or did she have a plan to find the statue?

A light came on in the back room. Kitty hurried along the rows of cages. She passed hutches full of sleeping bunnies and wide awake hamsters, running in their wheels. Two parrots with beautiful green- and-red feathers were perched in a tall cage with their heads under their wings.

Kitty stopped in the office doorway.
Piles of shiny things covered the desk,
the chair, and the filing cabinets inside.

Every corner of the room was filled with glittering treasures—silver plates, strings of pearls, and jewels in every colour of the rainbow.

Kitty gaped. All these treasures must be stolen! Was the robber dog really doing all this?

'Purr-fect greetings!' trilled a high voice.

Kitty jumped. The cat with the golden eyes lay on a pile of shiny coins. She was honey-coloured all over and the name *Precious* was spelled out on her collar in diamonds. Her pointed ears pricked up as Kitty walked in. There was an odd look in her golden eyes, as if she was trying to puzzle Kitty out.

'Hello, I'm Kitty!' said Kitty. 'I'm looking for a tiger statue. The springer spaniel that stole it came through your door just a few minutes ago.'

Precious

The cat's eyes gleamed and her tail flicked to and fro. 'My name is Precious. You must be the girl with superpowers that I've heard so much about. I bet your talents are very useful indeed!'

Kitty frowned. There was something strange about this cat. 'I try to use my powers to help others. That's why I'm looking for the Golden Tiger statue. It was taken from the museum tonight and it's very special! Did you see the robber dog that came in here?'

Precious cast a sideways look at

Kitty and began grooming herself. 'No, I didn't see a thing.'

'But he came right inside!' Kitty watched Precious lick her paws and clean behind her ears. Suddenly, she had a brainwave. What if the dog wasn't in charge of the robbery at all? Precious seemed like a sly sort of cat. She was definitely the type to organize a secret mission to steal the museum's treasure.

Kitty gave Precious a stern look. 'I think you know a lot more about the statue than you've said.

Tell me where it is!'

Precious gave a tinkly laugh. 'Why should I? The Golden Tiger is mine now. It makes an excellent addition to my treasures. I *do* like shiny things!' She stretched out on top of the gold coins and gave an exaggerated yawn.

'But everyone's coming to see the new exhibition tomorrow!' exclaimed Kitty. 'They'll be so disappointed not to see the Golden Tiger—it's a very important statue.' She stopped herself from telling Precious about the legend that the statue could grant your heart's desire.

A cat like her might wish for something very selfish—something that hurt other people!

'They'll just have to be happy with the other things in the museum,' snapped Precious. 'Humans are such whiny creatures! All I've taken is one *tiny* statue. Can't they manage without it?'

Kitty glared at the golden-eyed cat. There was no point trying to reason with her! She edged forward, looking for the statue behind the pile of coins.

'Oh, don't bother trying to find it.'
Precious waved her paw airily at a grey
metal box that was fixed to the wall. 'I
locked it away in the safe. I shall take
it out later and gaze at the diamonds
before I take a nap.'

Kitty sprang over to the safe. It was shut tight and it had a lock in the bottom corner. Precious gave another tinkly laugh. Kitty swung round, saying crossly, 'Why does that dog steal things for you anyway? Don't you both know it's wrong?'

'He does anything I say.' Precious beamed. 'Everyone does once they look into my eyes . . . including you!' Her golden eyes widened and Kitty felt them drawing her in like a magnet. Precious spoke in a growly tone. 'Listen very carefully! You will forget that you ever met me. You will not remember this pet shop. You will leave now and never come here again.'

Kitty's head swam. For a moment she could hardly remember why she was there. Then she thought about how much she wanted to help Cleo and her eyes sharpened again. 'You may have hypnotized the springer spaniel but I don't think it works on me! Maybe it's because of my superpowers.'

'Huh!' Precious flounced down from the coin pile and turned her back on Kitty, settling herself on a velvet blanket.

Kitty thought quickly. It was obvious that Precious was much more dangerous than she'd first thought. If no one stopped the golden-eyed cat

she could make the dog steal more
and more treasure. She might even
hypnotize other animals and force them
to join in.

An idea popped into Kitty's head.
Maybe there was a way to use the
stories about the statue to help her.
Perhaps she could scare Precious into
giving back the treasure.

'There's something you don't
know about the Golden Tiger,' she
began. 'Stories say that the statue has
a terrible curse.'

Precious stopped grooming and pricked up her ears. 'Why would I care about that?'

'Because the curse says that if someone upsets the statue, it will send scary spirits to take revenge,' said Kitty.

Precious was silent for a moment. 'Do you think it's true?'

'I don't really know.' Kitty noticed the cat's tail swaying uneasily. She tried to think of some extra details to make the story more believable. 'But if it *is* true, I expect the spirits come in the dead of night and creep in through tiny cracks around the door frame.' She shivered. That would be so spooky if it were true!

Precious sat up straight, her tail flicking faster and faster. 'Spirits? Door frames?'

There was a bang followed by a

loud clatter from the front of the shop.

Kitty jumped. Maybe the curse *was* real!

'What was that?' Precious leapt across the room, grabbing Kitty's hand with both paws. 'Save me, Kitty. I'm not a bad cat really!'

'Stay close to me.' Kitty's heart pounded like a drum as she crept towards the doorway. She could hear the pets squeaking and fluttering, woken by the strange noises. Kitty dodged as a box of fish food toppled from the shelves. Then she leapt bravely into the room.

Chapter
6

Kitty jumped as a hamster ran under her legs. 'Someone's opened all the cages!' she gasped. 'The animals are escaping.'

The little hamster climbed the shelves, cheeping sharply. Then a pink-eared rabbit hopped across the shop counter. The green-and-red parrots flew out of their cage, squawking, 'Stop, thief!'

'The curse is coming true,' moaned Precious. 'I wish that horrible statue had never come here.'

Kitty spotted Cleo's face peeping out from behind a fish tank. Then the grey cat pushed a box of hamster food off the shelf.

Kitty understood at once. Cleo had caused all this chaos to make Precious believe the story about the curse. The museum cat must have been listening the whole time!

Precious ran around in circles, her pointy ears swivelling from side to side. There was another crash as Cleo knocked a stack of dog leads to the floor. Precious arched her back fearfully. 'Kitty, the spirits are here to take revenge. Oh, save me!'

Cleo ducked behind the fish tanks

as the golden-eyed cat ran around in a panic.

'Why don't I take the statue back to the museum?' suggested Kitty. 'That will stop the curse.'

'Yes, yes! I will give you the silly statue!' cried Precious. 'I never want to see it again.' Running to the safe, she twisted the lock and the door clicked open.

Kitty took out the Golden Tiger and it felt heavy in her hand. 'Don't worry, you're safe now,' she told Precious. 'But to be really sure, you should tell the dog to return all the other stolen things.'

'I promise I will,' said Precious, her eyes wide.

'And never use your hypnotism on him, or anyone else, again,' added Kitty.

Precious nodded eagerly. 'I'll be good from now on. Please don't let the curse get me!'

'Wait for me here. I'll make sure everything's safe,' Kitty told her, before running back into the pet shop.

With Cleo's help, she ushered most of the pets back into their cages.

There was a sharp knock at the window and Pumpkin's face appeared. 'Kitty, the dog is returning and someone has switched a light on upstairs!'

'Goodbye, Precious!' called Kitty. 'Remember what you promised.'

Kitty and Cleo hid in the shadows as the springer spaniel trotted back into the pet shop then darted out of the door.

Kitty held the Golden Tiger tightly. 'We did it!' she whispered. 'Cleo, you're the *best* guard cat a museum could ever have! You were so clever making all that mess so that Precious would worry about the curse.'

CLOSED

Cleo puffed out her chest. 'I could tell that cat wouldn't give the statue back easily, so I made it as noisy as possible! I couldn't have done it without you, Kitty. I wish I had someone as kind and loyal as you helping me all the time.'

Pumpkin and Figaro ran over to join them and Pumpkin eyed the statue worriedly. 'I know the curse is just a story . . . but maybe we should take the Golden Tiger back to the museum as quickly as we can!'

'Well said!' Figaro yawned and stretched. 'All this excitement is exhausting. Besides, my stomach is empty and I need a nice big supper.'

They climbed back up the metal fire escape to the rooftop. Running along the ridge of the roof, they jumped from building to building. The moon rose higher in the sky and the stars glittered.

Leaping to the top of the museum, Kitty stopped for a moment to look across the city. The night wind swirled

over the rooftop, making her cape
flutter.

'Bother!' cried Cleo. 'Stan
must have discovered that the
statue's missing.'

Kitty peered through the glass dome. Two men were leaning over the platform where the Golden Tiger had stood. One was wearing a dark blue guard uniform. The other man had a bald head which gleamed in the moonlight.

'Who's that other man?' asked Kitty.

'That's Mr Martinez, the head of the museum,' Cleo told her.

'What do we do now?' cried Pumpkin. 'We can't put the statue back

102

without them seeing us.'

Kitty frowned. 'I suppose we could explain everything . . . but they might blame the owners of the pet shop for what Precious did, and this wasn't their fault at all.'

Figaro twirled his jet-black whiskers. 'I may have an idea! Follow me.'

They followed Figaro through an upstairs window. Their steps echoed in the stillness as they climbed down the marble staircase. Ducking behind a pillar, they watched more museum staff run along the passageway towards the exhibition room.

'So many people—it feels like the whole city will be here soon.' Cleo flicked her tail. 'We'd better be fast!'

'This way!' Figaro scampered into the museum restaurant and stopped beside a row of mouth-watering cakes, each displayed under a glass cake stand.

'What's your plan, Figaro?' asked Kitty.

Figaro waved his paw at a beautiful vanilla and blackcurrant cake with sugar frosting. 'As we cannot return the statue to its rightful place, we need to put it somewhere it will be found immediately in the morning. If we place it here, people will spot it straightaway.

I suggest using the empty chocolate cake stand.'

Kitty looked along the row, past the lemon cake with the white icing. At the end was an empty stand labelled *chocolate cake*, which had a scattering of deep-brown crumbs.

'You're right!' Cleo nodded approvingly at Figaro. 'Many visitors and staff come to have a morning coffee and a slice of cake and they'll spot the statue right away.' She jumped up on to the counter and lifted the lid of the cake stand with her teeth.

Kitty placed the Golden Tiger carefully underneath. Remembering the legend, she wondered if the statue knew her heart's desire. She touched its paw, and for a second the tiger's emerald eyes glowed in the dim light. Kitty smiled to herself and a tingle ran down her back.

Cleo replaced the lid of the cake stand. 'Quickly! We mustn't be found here.'

Kitty paused for a moment as the others darted back to the corridor. Finding a pencil behind the counter, she scribbled a message on a waiter's pad:

Here is the Golden Tiger which was stolen but returned safely thanks to Cleo the museum cat. 🐾

Smiling, she left the piece of paper beside the statue and ran to join the others.

By the time they reached the rooftop, the clock on the clock tower was chiming midnight.

'Thank you all so much.' Cleo bowed deeply. 'Kitty, I will never forget the help you gave me. You are a true friend!'

'I'll come and visit you when my mum and dad bring me to the museum,' promised Kitty. 'They'll love the story of how we saved the statue!'

Kitty, Pumpkin, and Figaro made their way home across the rooftops in the moonlight. Pumpkin brushed against Kitty's legs. 'Kitty, did you touch the Golden Tiger's paw?'

Kitty smiled at the little ginger cat. 'Yes I did! Just before I left it on the cake stand.'

Pumpkin skipped around a chimney pot. 'What's your greatest wish? Do you think it will come true?'

'*My* greatest wish would be for a delicious slice of salmon cooked in a garlic and herb sauce,' Figaro put in.

'I thought I'd wish for rubies and diamonds, but my wish wasn't for me— it was for Cleo. I hope the museum's grateful for everything she's done and they make her an official guard.' Kitty stopped to gaze at the beautiful night sky and the city lights winking in the darkness. Then she looked at Figaro and Pumpkin. 'Anyway, I have my greatest wish already. Being here with my friends is the best adventure in the world!'

Super facts about Cats

Super Speed

Have you ever seen a cat make a quick escape from a dog? If so, you'll know that they can move *really* fast—up to 30mph!

Super Hearing

Cats have an incredible sense of hearing and can swivel their large ears to pinpoint even the tiniest of sounds.

Super Reflexes

Have you ever heard the saying 'cats always land on their feet'? People say this because cats have amazing reflexes. If a cat is falling, they can sense quickly how to move their bodies into the right position to land safely.

Super Leaps

A cat can jump over eight feet high
in a single leap, this is due to its powerful
back leg muscles.

Super Vision

Cats have amazing night-time vision. Their
incredible ability to see in low light allows them
to hunt for prey when it's dark outside.

Super Smell

Cats have a very powerful sense of smell,
14 times stronger than a human's. Did you know
that the pattern of ridges on each cat's nose
is as unique as a human's fingerprint?

Kitty

and the
Sky Garden Adventure

Kitty

and the
Sky Garden Adventure

Girl by day. Cat by night. Ready for adventure

Written by **Paula Harrison** • Illustrated by **Jenny Løvlie**

Here's a taste of what's to come . . .

Kitty, Pumpkin, and Pixie discover a
secret sky garden on the city rooftops.

It's a wondrous place, filled with
exotic plants and beautiful decorations. Pixie is
so excited that she wants to tell the world about it,
but the more cats that learn of the secret garden,
the wilder it becomes. Soon Kitty has to step in
to rescue the garden and its beauty from those
who seem intent on destroying it.

About the author

Paula Harrison

Before launching a successful writing career,
Paula was a Primary school teacher. Her years teaching
taught her what children like in stories and how
they respond to humour and suspense. She went on
to put her experience to good use, writing many
successful stories for young readers.

About the illustrator

Jenny Løvlie

Jenny is a Norwegian illustrator, designer,
creative, foodie, and bird enthusiast. She is fascinated
by the strong bond between humans and animals and
loves using bold colours and shapes in her work.

Love Kitty?
Why not try these too . . .